A Cool Kid -Like Me!

A Cool Kid -Like Me!

Hans Wilhelm

Crown Publishers, Inc.
New York

For Sheila B.

Published by Crown Publishers, Inc., a Random House company,
225 Park Avenue South, New York, New York 10003
CROWN is a trademark of Crown Publishers, Inc.
Manufactured in the United States of America

Library of Congress Cataloging-in-Publication Data
Wilhelm, Hans. A cool kid—like me!/Hans Wilhelm.   p.   cm. Summary: A
young boy who is "cool" on the outside has some inner fears that he
expresses to his grandmother. ISBN 0-517-57821-2 (trade)—ISBN 0-517-57822-0
(lib. bdg.) [1. Self-confidence—Fiction. 2. Grandmothers—Fiction.] I. Title.
PZ7.W64816Co 1990   [E]—dc20   89-49370 CIP AC

10 9 8 7 6 5 4 3 2 1

First Edition

This story is about a kid everyone
thought was so terrific and so cool.
That kid was me.

I knew how to draw
great pictures.

I even brushed my teeth—
most of the time.

And I had a few friends to play with.

My parents left me alone a lot.
They thought I was a cool kid.
But that was only on the outside.
They didn't really know me.

Nobody knew what I was really like on the inside—except my grandma.

She wanted to know how I felt. "What's the matter?" she asked.

And I told her everything, like how scared I was without a night-light or how awful I felt when I dropped the ball.

I liked talking to Grandma. She was a good listener. And I could ask her all kinds of questions. Grandma was the only one I would let hug me.

One day she left for a long vacation.
But before she went, she gave me
a special present.

It was a teddy bear!

"Oh, no," said my father. "He's too old for that! He's a big boy now!"

"I agree," said my mother, shaking her head. "He won't play with it. He's already into computers."

What a weird present for a cool kid, I thought.

"Nonsense!" replied Grandma. "Nobody is too old for a teddy! It will keep him company while I am away."

Then I took another look at Teddy and decided that I liked him—except for the stupid ribbon, of course.

He was soft and cuddly
and kind of fun to hold.

I took him with me when I was
sure nobody could see him.

But when my mother cleaned
my room, she put him away
at the top of the closet.

"What was Grandma
thinking! You're too big
for this," she insisted.

But I took him down as soon
as she left the room.

Grownups think it's fun to be a
kid. But it's not fun all the time.
And that's what I talked about
with Teddy before we went to
sleep. He was the only one who
knew how I felt.

Teddy understood when I told him…

that I didn't like to be alone in the dark.

Teddy knew I was scared that I
would never have a best friend.

I could tell him I was afraid the other kids wouldn't like me and would laugh behind my back.

I was scared that I'd be picked last at games…

or that my parents would chew
me out in front of my friends.

Teddy knew how I felt when my parents were fighting…

or not talking to
each other at all.

And Teddy knew I was scared that my mother would leave and never come back! I know it was stupid, but sometimes I just could not help being scared.

There were other secrets, too,
that I could share with Teddy.
It made us feel much better.
Finally we would fall asleep.

In the morning things
wouldn't look so bad.
I would get ready to be
that cool kid again—
the one everyone
thought was so
terrific.

I would be as cool as I could be.
Except, of course...

when Grandma came home again.
    Boy, was I happy!
    On the outside *and* on the inside, too!